ONE CAMEL CALLED
DOUG

For Helen – a tango, as promised
(& I got a tree in, too!) – LF

To everyone who has really needed
a bit of 'me time' lately – SW

SIMON & SCHUSTER
First published in Great Britain in 2022 by Simon & Schuster UK Ltd
1st Floor, 222 Gray's Inn Road, London WC1X 8HB

A CIP catalogue record for this book is available from
the British Library upon request

ISBN: 978-1-4711-9145-9 (HB)
ISBN: 978-1-4711-9198-5 (PB)
ISBN: 978-1-4711-9146-6 (eBook)

Printed in Italy
1 3 5 7 9 10 8 6 4 2

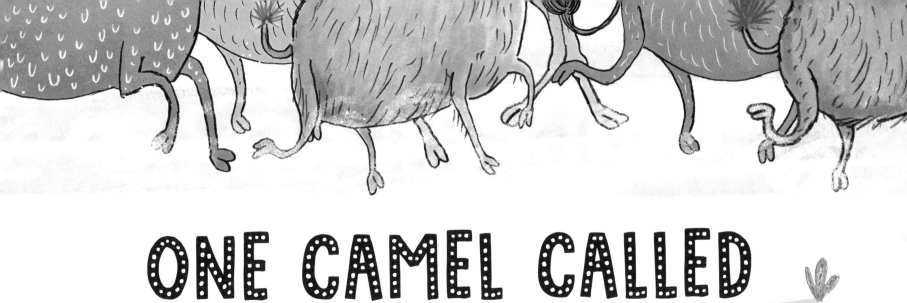

ONE CAMEL CALLED
DOUG

LU FRASER & SARAH WARBURTON

SIMON & SCHUSTER
London New York Sydney Toronto New Delhi

Under **one** sun in **one** far away land,
Where **one** desert wind whispers over the sand,
There's **one** bendy palm tree and **one** picnic rug

And one hump on the back of one camel called Doug.

"Hmmm,"
frowned Doug,
"all I can see,
Comes in a **one** …

and that includes ME!

And what if a **one** is
not quite enough?

It makes playing
hide-and-seek
terribly tough!"

found me

But, LOOK! Through the haze and the shimmering heat,
Plods a shadowy shape on squashy-toed feet.

"What's that," gasped Doug,
"is it a lion?" . . .

... No!

It's the
bump of a **hump**
of a camel
called Brian!

"Oh, think of the wonderful things we can do
If we stand side-by-side and our one becomes

... two!

TWO can play see-saw and leapfrog with ease.

TWO camels can tango or fly the trapeze!"

But, LOOK!

Through the haze and the shimmering heat,
Plods a shadowy shape on squashy-toed feet.

"What's that," cried Brian, "is it a bear?" ...

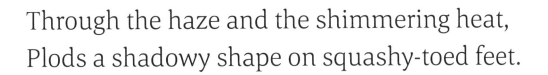

. . . No!

It's the
bump of a **hump**
of a camel
called Claire!

"Oh, it was amazing with you and with me,
But think of the things we can do now we're

... three!

You swing the skipping rope,
I'll do the jumps!
Oh, the marvellous things
we can do with **three** humps!"

But, LOOK!

Through the haze and
the shimmering heat,
Plods a shadowy shape
on squashy-toed feet.

"What's that," frowned Claire, "is it a moose?" ...

... No!

It's the
bump of a hump
of a camel
called Bruce!

"Oh, **three** is tremendous but add just one more,
And think of the things we can do now we're

. . . four!

Four can run relays
against the baboons.

Four fills a bobsleigh to swoosh
through the dunes!"

But, LOOK!

Through the haze and the shimmering heat,
Plods a shadowy shape on squashy-toed feet.
"What's that," shrieked Bruce, "is it a cheetah?" . . .

. . . No!
It's the
bump of a hump
of a camel
called Rita!

"Well, four was fantastic but now you've arrived,
Our humps make a furry phenomenal

. . . five!

Yes, five is a football team,
shooting and spinning!

Five football camels are scoring and winning!

But . . . STOP!" yelled Doug.
"Could it be?
That's ABSURD! . . .

OF A WHOLE

CAMEL HERD!

Oh! Think of the things we can do and can be
With **many** more camels," Doug sang,

"than just . . . ME!

One . . .

became two,

became **three,**

became
four,

And **four** becomes **five** when
there's **one** camel more!

And now we're a CROWD of
squashy-toed mammals,
We're a flock, we're a fleet, we're a . . .

Tune up the tubas! It's musical bumps! . . .

... Then we're fancy dress camels with glittery humps!

Quick! Pass the parcel! Where will it stop?...

... Then it's cactus piñata!
Watch the treats drop!

Now pick up your party bags! Form a neat line!
Humps at the ready, it's ...

TREASURE-HUNT TIME!

And into the sunset they sped with a shout.
"But I can't," whispered Doug . . .

"I'M ALL CAMELLED OUT!"

THWUMP! went Doug as he plopped on the sand,
And a camel-free peacefulness rolled through the land.

Then, "OH!" he cried from the spot where he'd flopped.
"Look at the stars I can see now I've stopped!

With **one** silver moon, high above, gently gleaming,
One swaying hammock for end-of-day dreaming,

One fluffy blanket, one teddy, one book,
There's a wonderful **oneness** wherever I look!

One pillow, one home, waiting under one tree . . .

For **one** bump of **one** hump of **one** camel

... just ME!

Yes, a herd full of humpity-camels is fun,
But SOMETIMES it's great being . . .